FAITH H. HAMLIN, LITERARY AGENT
SANFORD J. GREENBURGER ASSOCIATES
55 FIFTH AVENUE (15th FLOOR)
NEW YORK, NY 10003
(212) 206-5607

MY MOTHER THE CAT

MY MOTHER THE CAT

KATHERINE POTTER

SIMON & SCHUSTER BOOKS FOR YOUNG READERS

Published by Simon & Schuster
New York · London · Toronto · Sydney · Tokyo · Singapore

SIMON & SCHUSTER BOOKS FOR YOUNG READERS
Simon & Schuster Building, Rockefeller Center, 1230 Avenue of the Americas,
New York, New York 10020
Copyright © 1993 by Katherine Potter
All rights reserved including the right of reproduction in whole or in part in any form.
SIMON & SCHUSTER BOOKS FOR YOUNG READERS is a trademark of Simon & Schuster.
Designed by Lucille Chomowicz
The text of this book is set in Palatino.
The illustrations were done in pastels.
Manufactured in the United States of America   10   9   8   7   6   5   4   3   2   1

Library of Congress Cataloging-in-Publication Data
Potter, Katherine.
My mother the cat/by Katherine Potter.
Summary: When five-year-old Jane gets her wish to have her mother
switch places with her cat Puff, the resulting freedom to do
anything she wants turns out to be less than perfect.
[1. Cats—Fiction.   2. Mothers and daughters—Fiction.
3. Wishes—Fiction.]   I. Title.
PZ7.P8524My   1993   [E]—dc20
92-17864
CIP
ISBN 0-671-79632-1

For Richard Margolis

Jane McPlumb, five years old, was sent to her room for giving her dinner to the cat. She had slipped it under the table when her mother wasn't looking. Puff, the cat, ate the whole thing. "You know I hate fish sticks!" she yelled to her mother.

"No chocolate mousse for you tonight!" replied Mrs. McPlumb.

Jane shut her eyes tightly and gave Puff a big squeeze. "I wish *you* were my mother," Jane said to Puff. "Then things would certainly be different around here."

The next morning, Saturday, Jane got out of bed and went to look for her mother. She found her fast asleep in the laundry basket, purring. Jane scratched her head, frowned, and walked to the kitchen.

Jane was surprised to see Puff busy at the stove. "Good morning!" she said to Jane. "Sleep well?" Jane grinned and said, "Very well, thank you." Then she sat down to a breakfast of chocolate mousse and cocoa.

When Puff noticed Mrs. McPlumb at the door, she cheerfully placed a plastic bowl on the floor. In it was Kitty De-Lite Liver Entree. Mrs. McPlumb ate the whole thing.

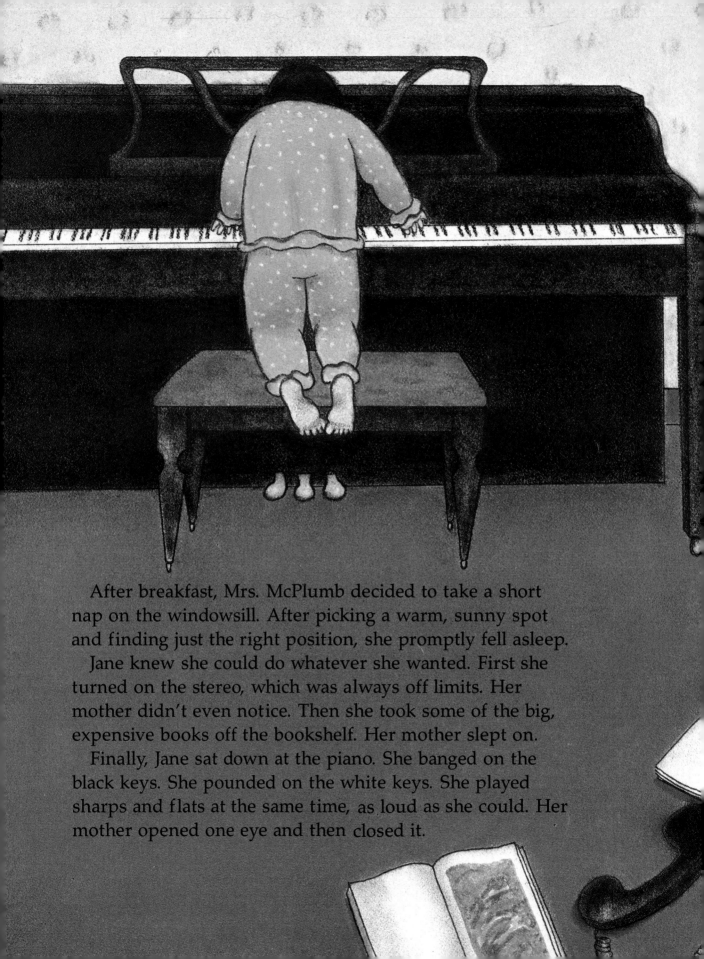

After breakfast, Mrs. McPlumb decided to take a short nap on the windowsill. After picking a warm, sunny spot and finding just the right position, she promptly fell asleep.

Jane knew she could do whatever she wanted. First she turned on the stereo, which was always off limits. Her mother didn't even notice. Then she took some of the big, expensive books off the bookshelf. Her mother slept on.

Finally, Jane sat down at the piano. She banged on the black keys. She pounded on the white keys. She played sharps and flats at the same time, as loud as she could. Her mother opened one eye and then closed it.

Next Jane turned on the television to a show her mother never let her watch. It was boring, but she watched it till the end, anyway, while eating an entire bag of potato chips.

Jane went to her mother's room.
She put on a party dress,

high-heeled shoes,

pearls, and some red, red lipstick,
which she also rubbed onto
her cheeks.

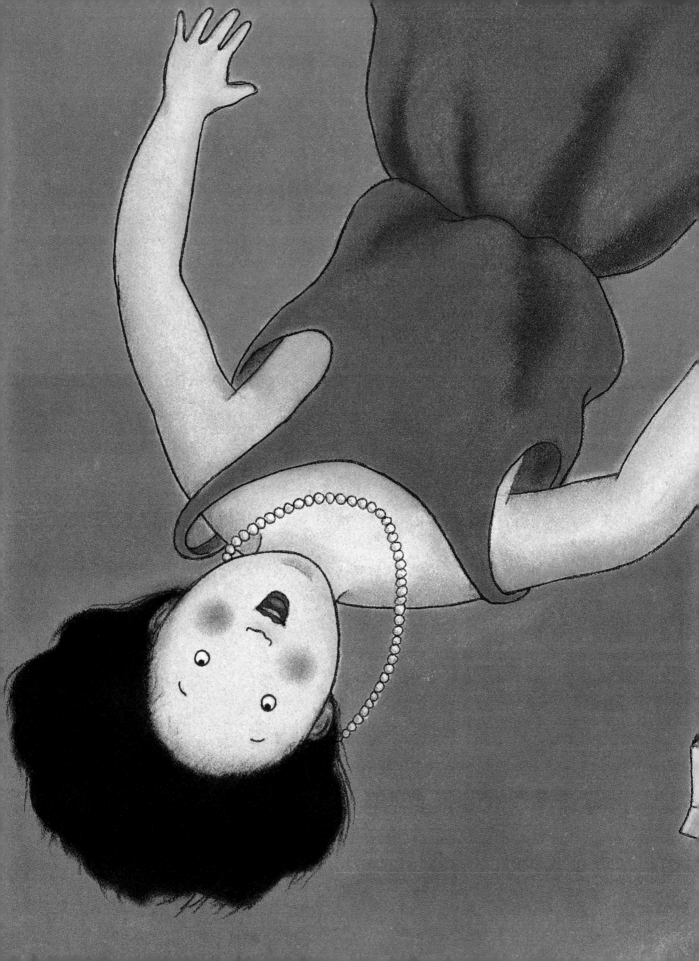

Jane danced around the room, jumped on the bed, and made faces at herself in the mirror; but it wasn't much fun without her mother there to scold her.

Jane was watching cartoons on television when Puff came in and announced, "Time to do the grocery shopping!"

"Oh, goody!" Jane said. "Can we buy some treats?"

"Sure!" Puff replied. "I've already got some in mind."

And off they went.

In the car, Jane wanted to listen to her favorite radio station, but Puff kept pushing the button and switching it back to a program called "Bird Talk."

At the market, Puff sped up and down the aisles, ignoring Jane's pleas for jelly beans and cookies. Puff finally found what she wanted: the fish department. "What's fresh today?" she asked the woman behind the counter.

On the way home, Jane was fuming. All they had bought were twelve pounds of swordfish and three gallons of whole milk.

Puff noticed Jane pouting and said, "Why don't we stop at the pet shop, dear?"

Once inside, Puff made a beeline for a cage full of mice. "We'll take these guys here," she said, pointing to two fat white rodents. "Or would you rather have a goldfish, Jane?"

Jane had a feeling the mice were *not* going to be her pets. By now she was very annoyed with Puff; and as soon as they got home, she ran to find her mother, hoping things would be back to normal.

But Mrs. McPlumb was in the living room, batting a catnip toy around and chasing after it.

Puff was in the kitchen scaling fish. "Time to eat!" she soon called to Jane.

Puff had prepared fish chowder, fish stew, fish salad, and broiled fish for dinner. And there was plenty of milk.
Jane wrinkled her nose. "I don't like it," she said.
"Fine!" Puff said, eating noisily.

Jane had jelly on bread, mint chocolate-chip ice cream, and lemonade instead.

Then Puff put a covered tray on the table. "Now for dessert!" she said.

"No thanks, I'm feeling sick," mumbled Jane. And she went to her room.

Even though it was half past eight, Jane's bedtime, she brought her pile of Rocket Girl comic books to bed, determined to read them all. She waited and waited for her mother to tell her to go to sleep, but nobody came.

Her eyelids drooping, Jane finally put her head on the pillow. But before turning off the light, she made a wish. "I want Mommy to be Mommy, and Puff to be Puff." She repeated these words until she fell asleep.

The first thing Jane did when she woke up was run into her mother's room. She got into bed and peered at her mother's face. "Morning, Mommy," she said.

Her mother opened her eyes, smiled, and said, "Good morning, darling." Then she gave Jane a big hug. "Now go wash up for breakfast. I'll make pancakes!"

Jane washed her face and hands, combed her hair, and even brushed her teeth before skipping into the kitchen. Puff was eating her Kitty De-Lite.

Mrs. McPlumb stretched and said, "My, I feel so rested!" When she saw the tray on the table, she said, "Hmm, what could this be?" Then she lifted the lid.